Alice in Wonderland

Down the Rabbit Hole

Alice in Wonderland

Down the Rabbit Hole

Joe Rhatigan & Charles Nurnberg
Illustrated by Eric Puybaret

ALICE

was *sitting* by the river having
an oh-so-ordinary afternoon, when
a White Rabbit
ran by.

Not just any old rabbit, but one
with **pink** eyes, a **red** jacket
and a great **big** pocket watch.

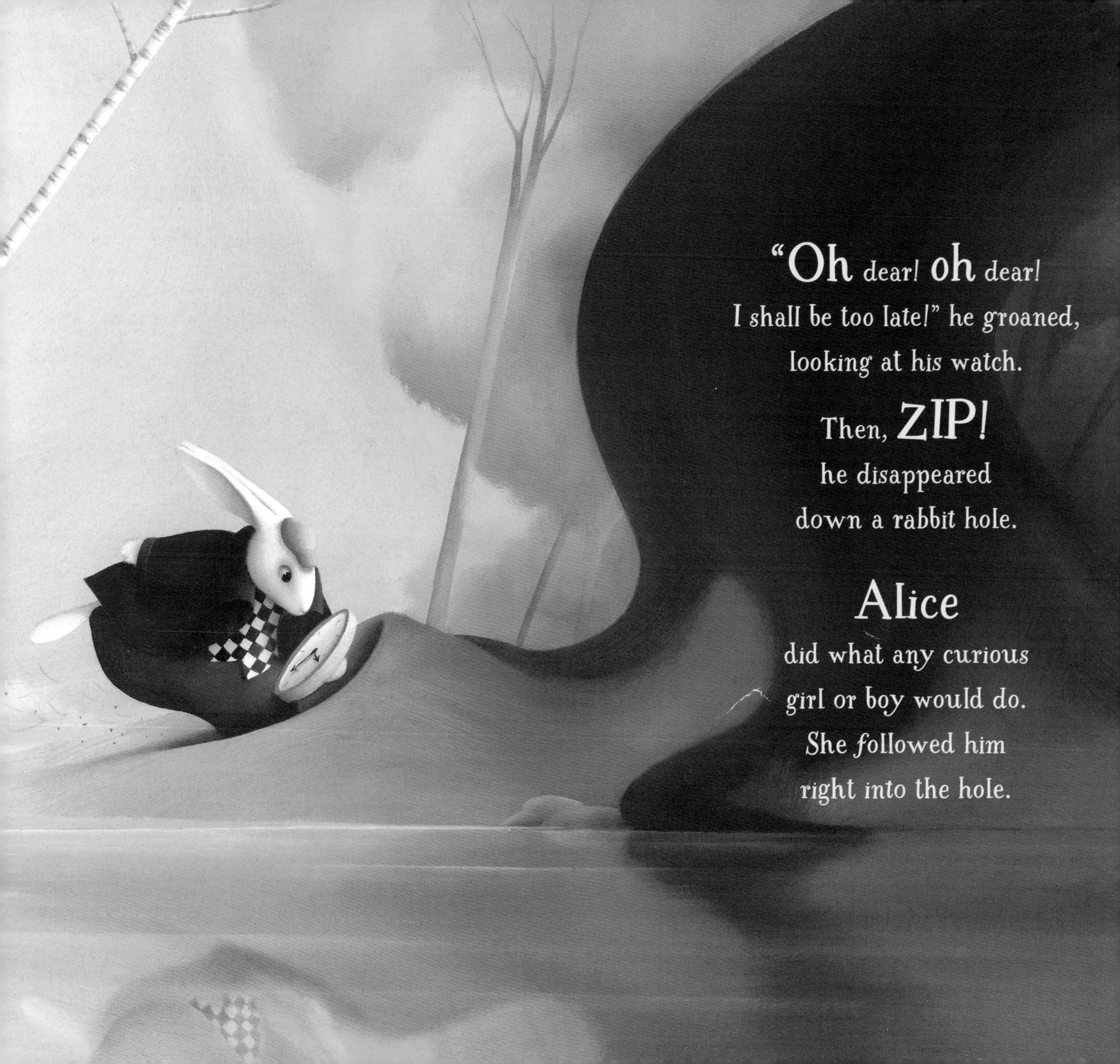

"Oh dear! oh dear!
I shall be too late!" he groaned,
looking at his watch.

Then, ZIP!
he disappeared
down a rabbit hole.

Alice
did what any curious
girl or boy would do.
She followed him
right into the hole.

DOWN, DOWN, DOWN she fell.
Alice fell for such a long,
long time that she thought she might
fall all the way through the earth.

Finally, THUMP, THUMP,
she landed softly on a pile of leaves
and sticks – not hurt at all.

And there was
the White Rabbit,
running down the hallway,
yelling,
"Oh my ears
and whiskers,
how late it's getting!"

The White Rabbit turned
a corner and simply disappeared.
Alice found herself alone in
a long hallway with lots and lots of doors.
On a table was a golden key – a key
that worked on one special, tiny door.

That door opened into the most
beautiful garden Alice had ever seen,
with bright flowers and pretty fountains.
Alice longed to visit the garden.

But she was just too **big** to get
through that tiny door.

Perhaps there's a key to
a **bigger** door that will take
me to the garden,
Alice thought.

But *instead* of another key,
she *found* a bottle labelled

"DRINK ME".

She thought *for* a minute
and then did exactly that.

"What a curious *feeling*,"
Alice cried,
as *she got* smaller and smaller.
"I can *fit* through the door now!"

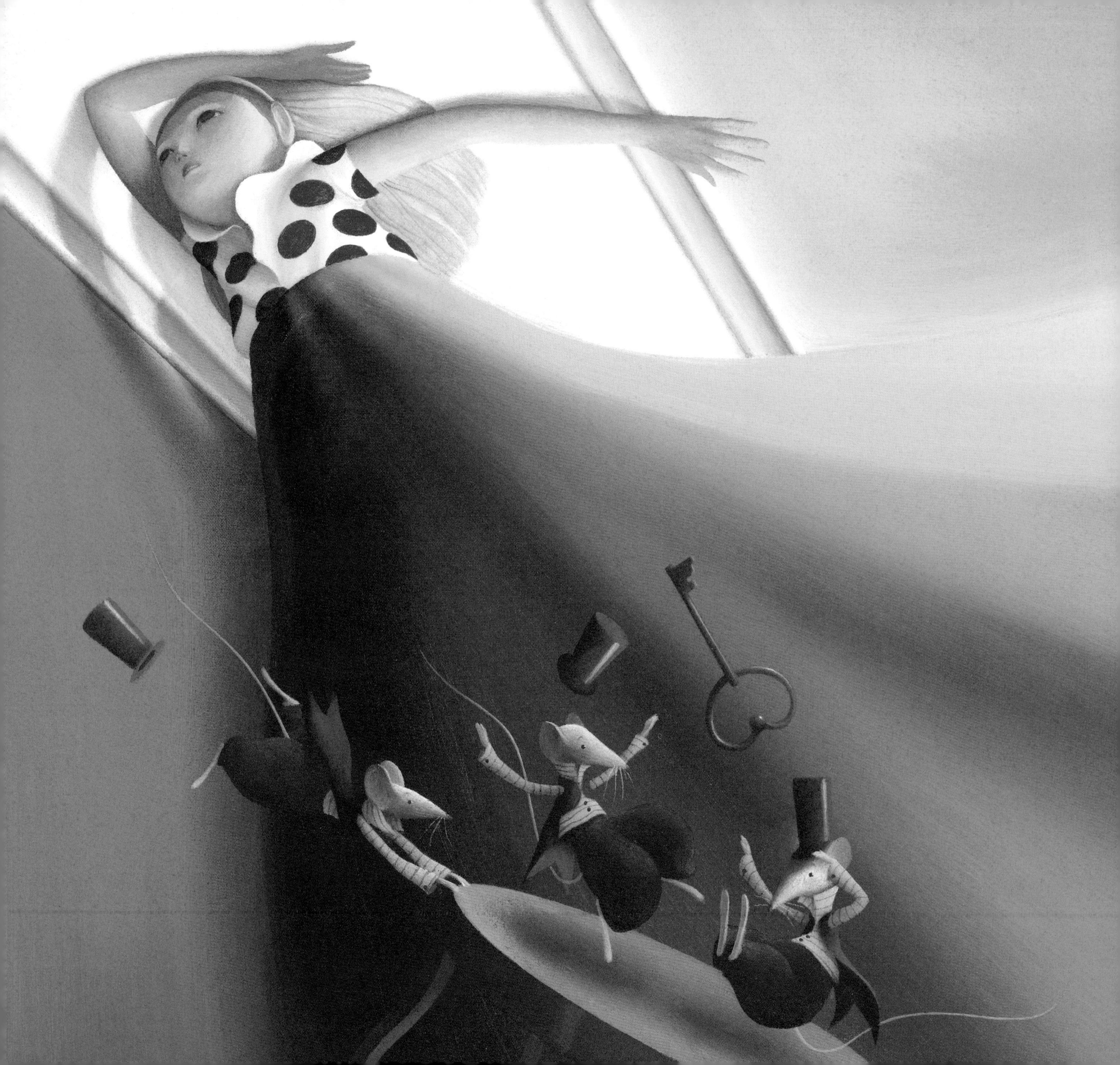

UH OH.

Alice was now so small she
couldn't reach the golden key,
which she had left on the table.

But under the table Alice *found*
a box with a tiny cake labelled

"EAT ME".

She thought *for* a minute
and then did exactly that.

Suddenly,
Alice began to grow

TALLER.

"CURIOUSER AND
CURIOUSER!" cried Alice.

"GOODBYE, FEET!"

“Now there’s no way
I can fit through that tiny door,”
Alice cried.

Buckets of tears fell down
her cheeks, making a big puddle.

ZOOM!

The White Rabbit ran by.
The very **big Alice** scared him,
and he dropped his fan and gloves
and disappeared.

Alice grabbed the fan, which made
her tiny again – so tiny she fell into her river
of tears. She swam and swam,
and soon met up with Mouse,
Duck, Eaglet, Dodo, and a lot of
other interesting animals.

Everyone swam to shore
to dry off by having a race.

Round and round they went until
they were all quite dry.

Alice,

who by now was beginning
to miss her home, said,
"I wish I had my Dinah here.
She's my cat and she's great
at catching mice.
And you should
see her chase the birds."

WOW!

That scary thought
sent all the animals
running off.

"WAIT!
What's that sound?
Footsteps?"

It was the White Rabbit again!
"Run home this minute and
get my gloves and fan,"
he told Alice.

Alice ran and *found* the house
and the *gloves* and *fan inside* . . .
and a *special* bottle too.

"I know *something interesting*
is bound to happen,"
she said as *she* drank *from* it.

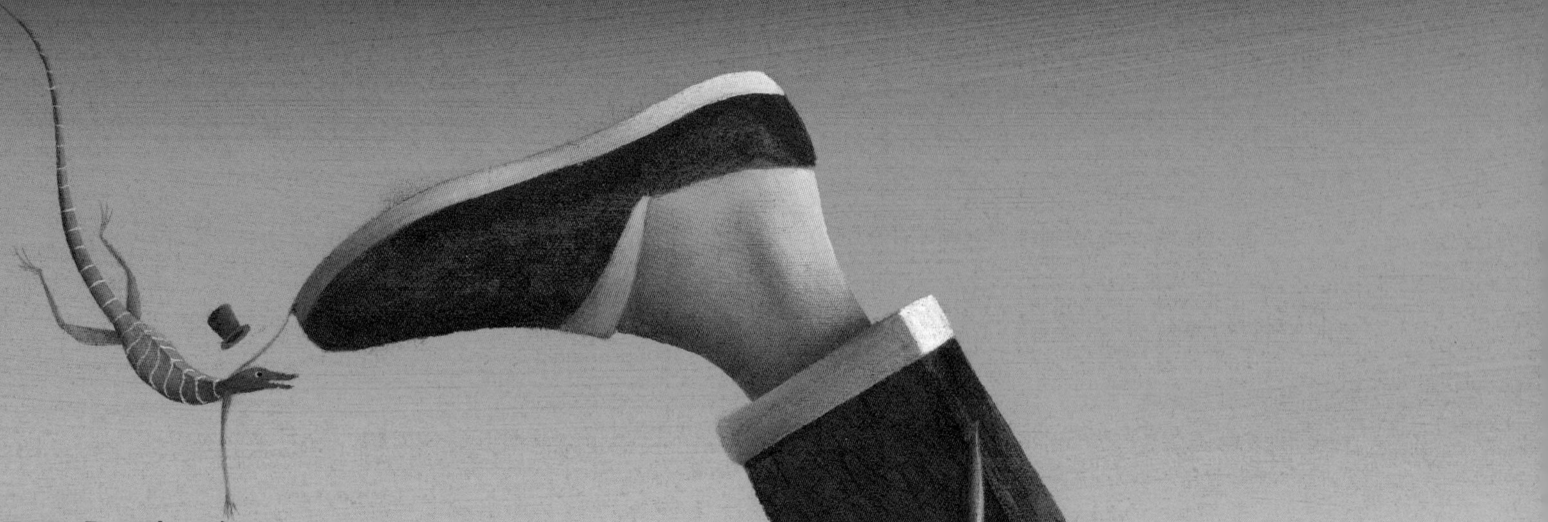

"YIKES! I'm growing."

Alice's head pushed against the ceiling, her *foot* went up the chimney, and an arm stuck out a window.

Frightened by what had happened to Alice, the White Rabbit and his animal friends sent Bill the Lizard down the chimney to see what was going on.

Alice gave him a little kick.

"There goes Bill!" Alice heard the animals say.

"CATCH HIM!"

The White Rabbit,
Dodo, Mouse and all the animals
surrounded the house,
throwing pebbles at
GIANT Alice.

Every stone turned into a small,
magical cake when it hit her.

"I bet I know what will happen if
I eat one,"
Alice said to herself.

Sure enough, after swallowing a cake,
she was soon small enough to
race out the door and escape.

Tiny **Alice** needed something special to eat to get back to her regular girl size. And then she needed to find her way home.

She saw a **giant** mushroom with a

Blue Caterpillar

sitting right on top.

"Eat the mushroom," he said. "One side of it will make you smaller and the other **bigger**."

One bite and **Alice**'s chin almost hit her feet.

A bite from the other side and her neck grew so **LONG** her head was soon lost in the clouds.

A few more bites and she finally got to the right size. **Phew!**

"HOW PUZZLING

all these changes are," Alice said to herself. "But now that I'm my right size, I wonder how I can get back to the riverbank and to my cat and my home?"

All **Alice** could do was walk on, knowing only that whatever happened next, it certainly was bound to be

not ordinary at all.

For Axel, Ariane, and their children. - E. P.

To Barbara, the love of my life, for all we are together.
And to my three little princesses, Alexis, Casey and Mackenzie,
who bring me joy and happiness every day in so many
ways they cannot imagine. - C. N.

You were my boss, mentor and publisher. Now you are my
collaborator and friend. Thank you, Charlie, for believing in
this project and believing in me. - J. R.

Illustrator's Note

I'm under the impression that we all have a personal story with Alice. She seems so familiar. My own personal connection to Alice is the way she's always surprised by what happens to her; she always marvels, just like me. In fact, I think we all live in Wonderland and simply don't realize it. We just have to let ourselves be surprised by the wonders of our world. - E. P.

About Lewis Carroll

Charles Lutwidge Dodgson (1832–1898), better known by his pen name, Lewis Carroll, was born in Daresbury, Cheshire. The third of eleven children, Dodgson proved himself an entertainer at a young age, performing plays and giving readings for his many siblings. He was also known for his intellect, and went on to win many academic prizes in school, especially for mathematics. A master of word play, logic puzzles, and later, photography, Dodgson is best known for his two books following the incredible adventures of a young girl named Alice. Begun as a way to entertain three little girls on a boating trip in 1862, today *Alice's Adventures in Wonderland* (1865) and *Through the Looking-Glass* (1872) are among the most quoted works of literature, with unforgettable characters permanently entrenched in our culture.

First published in the USA 2015 by Imagine Publishing, Inc.
This edition published 2015 by Macmillan Children's Books,
an imprint of Pan Macmillan
20 New Wharf Road, London N1 9RR
Associated companies throughout the world
www.panmacmillan.com

ISBN: 978-1-4472-8623-3

3 5 7 9 8 6 4

A CIP catalogue record for this book is available from the British Library.

Printed in Belgium

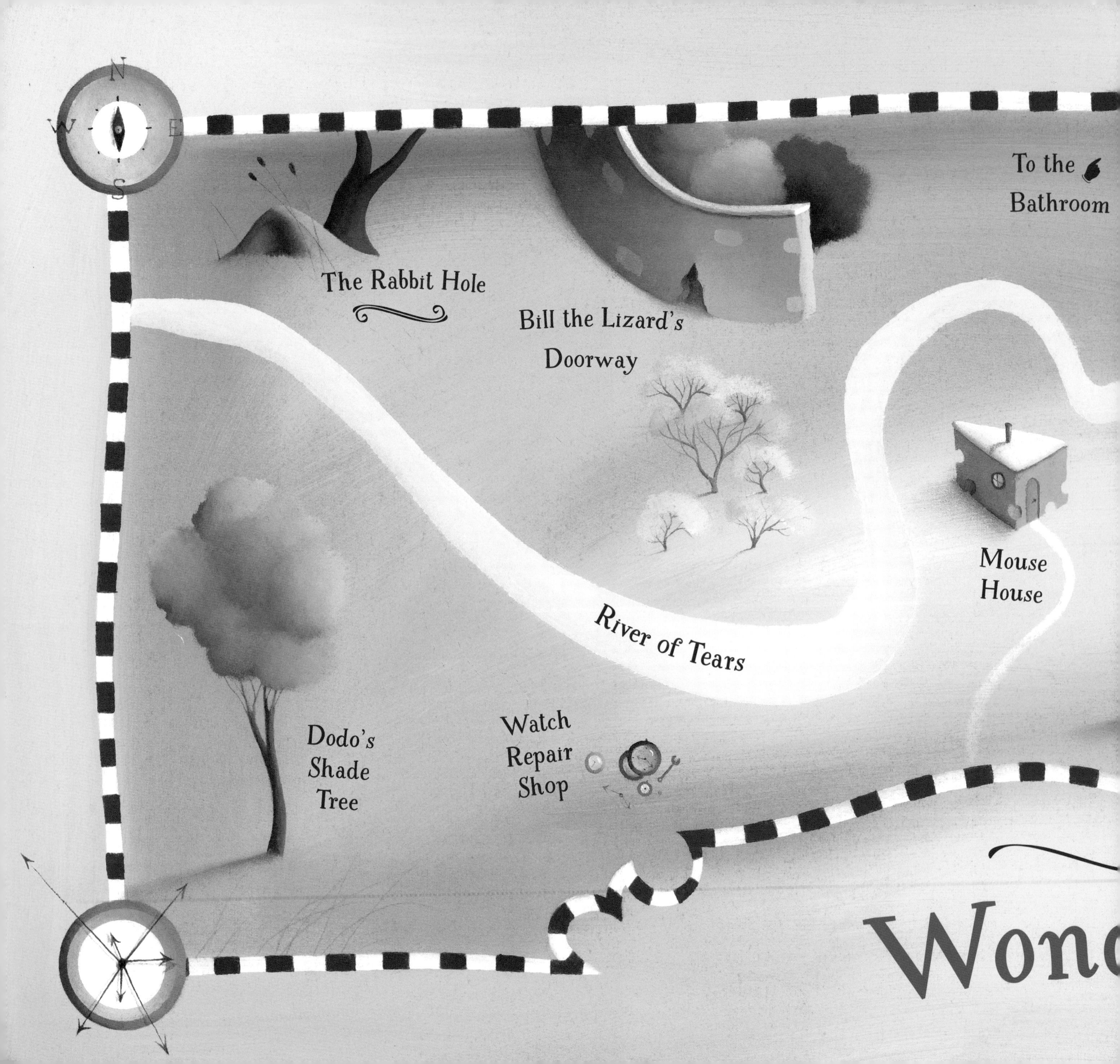
N
W
E
S
To the Bathroom
The Rabbit Hole
Bill the Lizard's Doorway
Mouse House
River of Tears
Dodo's Shade Tree
Watch Repair Shop
Wond

Carrot Forest
To the Tea Party
Magical Cupcake Bakery
River of Tears
The White Rabbit's House
Blue Caterpillar Place
erland
N
W
E
S

More magical stories from Eric Puybaret

ISBN: 978-0-230-70381-0

ISBN: 978-0-230-75029-6

Each book comes with a bonus CD of enchanting music for you to enjoy again and again.